This Puffin Book

belongs to

_____

_____

Tick the
Puffin Nibbles
you have read!

BAD BUSTER
Sofie Laguna
Illustrated by Leigh Hobbs

FIRST FRIEND
Christobel Mattingley
Illustrated by Craig Smith

MY AMAZING POO PLANT
Moya Simons
Illustrated by Judith Rossell

NO CAT – AND THAT'S THAT!
Bruce Dawe
Illustrated by Andrew McLean

THE MERMAID'S TAIL
Raewyn Caisley
Illustrated by Ann James

TOPSY AND TURVY
Justin D'Ath
Illustrated by Emma Quay

Visit us at puffin.com.au

Puffin Nibbles

My Amazing Poo Plant

WITHDRAWN

Moya Simons

Illustrated by **Judith Rossell**

Puffin Books

For Shayli and Chasen Green with love   *M.S.*
For Kit, Paul, Tim and Patrick   *J.R.*

PUFFIN BOOKS

UK | USA | Canada | Ireland | Australia
India | New Zealand | South Africa | China

Penguin Random House Australia is part of the Penguin Random House group of companies whose
addresses can be found at global.penguinrandomhouse.com.

First published by Penguin Books Australia in 2005
This edition published by Puffin Books, an imprint of
Penguin Random House Australia Pty Ltd, in 2019

Text copyright © Moya Simons 2005
Illustrations copyright © Judith Rossell, 2005

The moral right of the author and illustrator has been asserted.

Design by Melissa Fraser and Tony Palmer
© Penguin Random House Australia Pty Ltd
Typeset in New Century School Book by
Post Pre-press Group, Brisbane, Queensland

Printed and bound in Australia by Griffin Press, part of Ovato, an accredited
ISO AS/NZS 14001 Environmental Management Systems printer

 A catalogue record for this
book is available from the
National Library of Australia

ISBN 978 014 330146 2. (Paperback)

Penguin Random House Australia uses papers that are natural and recyclable
products, made from wood grown in sustainable forests. The logging and
manufacture processes are expected to conform to the environmental
regulations of the country of origin.

penguin.com.au

Chapter one

I live in a third-floor
apartment. I asked Mum
if I could have a pet.

She smiled and said,
'What about a pot plant?
They make great pets.'

Once we had a dog. He

was little and yapped all
night. I used to take him
for walks, but when it
rained he yapped all day.

The neighbours
complained. They said
'You can't keep a dog in an
apartment.' We had to give

him to an old man living down the street who was a bit deaf. It was very sad.

'Pot plants don't yap,' said Mum.

We once had a cat, but one day she jumped from the balcony onto a moving truck. We never saw her again. She might be on her way to the Simpson Desert. It's very sad.

'Pot plants don't jump

onto moving trucks,'
said Mum.

A friend of mine had a
guinea pig. The guinea

pig ran up and down the
balcony. And in and out
of the hallway. And up
and down the kitchen. He
left little soft dark pellets

behind in a very cute trail.

I thought it was wonderful.

My friend could always find

him when he got lost.

My mum said, 'A guinea

pig? No way! Pot plants give you no trouble.'

I asked for Mexican Walking Fish – big mistake.

One day they had a fish argument. The yellow fish bit the legs off the black fish. Then (gulp) he ate them (yuck). We took the fish to a pond and waved as they swam away (in different directions).

'Pot plants don't eat each other,' said Mum.

Chapter Two

Now I have no pets at all.
I'm standing on my balcony.
There's just me and Mum's
forty-five pot plants. My
mum has a thing about
pot plants.

'They make great pets,'

she tells me. 'All they
need is sunshine, water, a
sprinkle of plant food and
a nice chat.'

Mum loves to talk to her
pot plants. 'Hello there,
Jemima,' she says to
the petunia pot plant.

'My, you're looking great.'
The petunia wriggles
in the wind and its petals
uncurl.

'That's a petunia smile,' my mum tells me. Then she says, 'Hi,' to Rebecca the Rose, and Cathy the Carnation.

'Why don't you have your very own pot plant?' asks Mum. 'It would make a lovely pet. Look, I have this empty pot full of earth where Dina my daisy lived, before she died and went to daisy heaven.'

'I *don't* want a pot plant for a pet,' I tell Mum, and I stamp my foot to let her know I am very serious.

Suddenly, a large bird
sweeps low over the
balcony. I can hear his
dark wings flutter as he

flies right by me. Then, plop, a big white dropping falls into the empty pot. It sits on the dark earth like mushy vanilla ice-cream.

'Oh, yuck, yuck, yuck,' I say and I shudder to show I am really serious.

Mum studies the white, gooey plop. 'What an interesting shape,' she says. 'I've seen a painting just like that in the art gallery.'

Then she adds, 'I'd better
water it right away.'

I'm very worried. Is my
mum going potty? 'Why do

you want to water a
bird poo?'

'Emma,' she says to
me. 'Birds eat all kinds

of things, so they carry
amazing bits and pieces in
their droppings. Now that
bird *could* be carrying the

seed of some wonderful
flower. If we don't water
the poo we'll never find out.
First of all though, we need
to bury it.'

How embarrassing.
First, my mum takes a
small spade and covers
the poo with earth. Then
she waters it. Oh, and now
she's talking to it!

'Dear little poo plant,
I hope you grow into a

wonderful flower.' Then
Mum says to me, 'Emma,
why don't you make the poo
plant your new pet?'

Well, there's no way that

I'm going to make a *poo*
plant my new pet. Why
would I do that?

But then I think some
more. My friends have cats,

dog, mice and birds. One
friend even has a blue-
tongue lizard. But not one
of my friends has ever had
a poo plant. I'd be the only

person I know who has a poo plant for a pet. That is, of course, if the bird poo does grow into a plant.

So, I say to Mum, 'Okay, the poo plant can be *my pet*. But are you sure that a plant is going to grow from that dropping?'

Mum smiles at me. 'There's only one way to find out.'

Chapter Three

That does it. Each day I
water the earth in the pot
plant, and watch. I give it
plant food for breakfast and
when no one is watching I
speak to it. 'Come on, do me
a favour, *grow*. Don't just

sulk. Turn into something
amazing.'

One week later, a tiny

green shoot appears.

I am so excited. I run to

the phone and tell all my

friends. 'I'm growing a poo plant, the world's first poo plant.' I tell them all about the bird, and the dropping.

My friends come over. They nearly trip over all the pot plants on the balcony. Finally I show them my poo plant, which is two tiny shoots in the earth of a red pot.

'It's not very interesting,' says Maisie. 'And how can

a poo plant be as good as a dog? You can't take a poo plant for a walk.'

'Yes, I can,' I reply, with

my nose in the air. 'I can put the poo plant in a basket and walk it all day long.'

'You can't pat it,' says
Darren.

'Can so,' I say, as I stroke
the tiny leaf of my poo
plant.

'How do you know that
your poo plant isn't going to
grow into a weed?'

Hmm. I haven't thought
about that. 'I just *know*,'
I say.

'Well,' says Maisie,
'I know one thing you

can't do. You can't enter
your poo plant in the school
pet show.'

My eyes begin to droop.

'I can so,' I say. But really I'm thinking the same thing. How can I enter my poo plant in a pet show? Everyone would just laugh.

chapter four

Our teacher at school, Mrs
Snellbottom, gives us a note
to take home. It's all about
the pet show. It costs two
dollars to enter your pet.
All the money raised will
help buy extra books for

our library. There are three sections: the cutest pet, the best-looking pet and the most unusual pet.

Maisie says she's going to
enter Fluffy. 'She's the best-
looking rabbit in the world.'
Darren says he's going

to enter his cat, Tiddles,
in the cutest pet section.
'I think the way she goes
cross-eyed makes her
extra cute.'

'I'm going to enter my poo
plant for the most unusual
pet,' I say bravely. 'I bet no
one else has a poo plant.'

My friends don't answer.
Maisie turns away, covering
her mouth with her hand.
Is she laughing at me?

I fill in the entry form.
Time passes. Soon it's just
two more days until the
pet show.

Mum is very encouraging.

'Your poo plant is growing taller and taller,' she says. Mum's right. There are shoots growing this way and that way and there

are tiny buds forming. It's
amazing how different the
shoots look to each other.
Is there a chance that my

poo plant could really be
a weed?

I start to shudder.

On the day of the pet
show, Mum makes a
special sign for my plant.
It says:

This is a Poo Plant. This
amazing plant grew from the
seeds in a poo dropped by a bird
into an empty pot of earth.
Isn't nature wonderful!

I am not so keen on
Mum's last words about
nature being wonderful.

But I guess that it's hard
to write beautiful things
about a poo.

chapter five

Mum and Dad come along
to the pet show. All the pets
are lined up. There are
dogs and cats and rabbits
and guinea pigs and a
mean-looking goat. There
are turtles and mice and

a big white rat and Jamie
has brought along a box of
worms. There's a duck and
a chicken and a lizard and

Michelle has brought along
her big pet spider.

First they have the cutest
pets contest. Some of these

pets aren't cute at all.
The big white rat tries to
bite the judge. In the end
Tiddles, the cross-eyed cat
wins. Tiddles meows then
makes a grab for a mouse
dressed up as a toy soldier
in the next cage.

Next they have the best-
looking pets. There are cats
that look like they've just
come from a kitty beauty
salon and dogs that are as

sleek as racehorses. Mary

Binley's pet lamb wins. Its

fleece really is as white as

snow, though it doesn't stay

that way for long. A tiny

dog chases the lamb onto

the grass, which is wet and
muddy from last night's
rain. Still, it doesn't matter

because the lamb has
already won a bright
blue ribbon.

I nervously line up
with all the others for the
most unusual pet contest.
There's Michelle, who has
her pet spider in a shoe
box. There's Jamie with
his box of long pink worms.
They are all tangled up
like spaghetti. Someone's
brought in a green and

orange caterpillar, and
Dave has brought along
his pet rock.

Chapter Six

I stand there beside my poo
plant. Kids read the sign,
point to my plant, and roll
around laughing. Their
parents laugh too. This is
very, very embarrassing.
My parents, who are

sensible, stand and smile
at me as the judge moves
from spider to worms, along
the line of very, very
unusual pets.

I look down at my poo

plant. It's really amazing
how it's grown. I see the
very first bud has opened
into a flower and on a lower
branch there's another
flower uncurling. 'Good

little poo plant,' I whisper,
'smile for the judge.'
    The judge says nice
things about all the

unusual pets, even the

worms. Then he stands

in front of my poo plant.

He reads Mum's note.

'A poo plant,' he says,

'well, I never!'

My knees are knocking

together as he has a close

look at my plant.

'Will you look at this!'

he says.

I start to worry. What is

he staring at?

'Amazing. Just amazing.'

Are there bugs crawling on my plant?

'Young lady,' he says to me. 'When I'm not being a judge, I have a plant nursery. Did you know that you have *three* different flowers growing in your poo plant? There's a geranium, a rose and even a sunflower. The seeds must have all mixed together in

the bird poo. Your poo plant
is very, very unusual.'

I am a star. I grin from
ear to ear. I can't lose.

I don't lose. I am given the
blue ribbon for the most
unusual pet!

I say nice things to my
poo plant all the way home.

I stroke it and give it extra plant food for dinner.

Now, when birds fly low over our balcony, I run after them with a pot full of earth. 'Do your poo here,' I call out to them.

I'm very hopeful. I could grow an apple-orange tree with a dash of banana. You just never know!

From Moya Simons

Anyone can grow a rose bush or a tomato vine, but a poo plant? After you've read this story, you'll know exactly how to grow your very own poo plant. All your friends will want to come and see it. How do I know so much about poo plants? Well, I've grown one myself – and that's how I came to write this story!

From Judith Rossell

I've always loved animals, and so I had fun drawing all the different pets in this story. I've never had a plant for a pet, but I like growing things. I grew a weed in the garden that was taller than me, and sometimes I grow interesting, furry things on the cheese in the fridge.

Want another Nibble?

POO PLANT

Being bad was what Buster
did best. Until his dad thought
of a way to sort him out.

Will Adam ever achieve his
dream of being an astronaut?

Becky only wants fairy bread at
her party. But there's so much left
over, and she won't throw it out.

Nicholas Nosh is the littlest pirate
in the world. He's not allowed to go
to sea, and he's bored. Very bored.
'I'll show them,' he says.

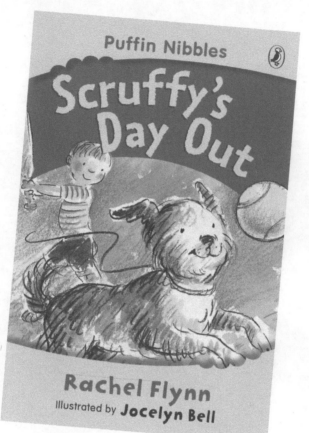

Puffin Nibbles

Scruffy's Day Out

Rachel Flynn
Illustrated by **Jocelyn Bell**

Dad saves a little scruffy dog
from being run over.
But who does it belong to?

Crystal longs to be a mermaid.
So her mother makes her a special
tail. But what will happen when
Crystal wears her tail to bed?

Find your story

puffin.com.au